Harvey, the Traveling Harmonica

What Children are Saying ...

My favorite picture was when Walter played tug-of-war with Buddy and Harvey. The funniest part was Harvey being in the wormy pocket.
—Becca, age 5

My favorite part was when Buddy saved Harvey. It was funny that he howled when Harvey was making music with the harmonica. I love the picture of Buddy saving Harvey from the water because he loved him.
—Bentley, age 6

The funniest part of this story is when Harvey is in the pocket with the worms. My favorite picture is when he's in the pocket with the candy.
—Landon, age 5

Harvey, the Traveling Harmonica

Becky Van Vleet

illustrated by Courtney Smith

This book is a work of fiction. Characters are the product of the author's imagination. Any resemblance to actual events or persons, living or dead, is entirely coincidental.

Cover and Interior Design: Courtney Smith, Derinda Babcock
Editor(s): Derinda Babcock, Deb Haggerty
Illustrated by: Courtney Smith
PUBLISHED BY: Elk Lake Publishing, Inc., 35 Dogwood Dr., Plymouth, MA 02360, 2020

Library Cataloging Data
Names: Van Vleet, Becky (Becky Van Vleet)
Harvey, the Traveling Harmonica / Becky Van Vleet
48 p. 21.6 cm × 21.6 cm (8.5 in. x 8.5 in.)
Identifiers: ISBN-13: 978-1-64949-072-8 (paperback) | 978-1-64949-073-5 (trade hardcover) | 978-1-64949-074-2 (trade paperback) | 978-1-64949-075-9 (e-book)
Key Words: Children, Early Learning, Family Life, Family Traditions, Family Customs, Harmonica, Friends
LCCN: 2020946050 Fiction

Author's Dedication

This book is dedicated in loving memory of my father, Walter, who inspired me to write this story. My childhood memories of his harmonica tunes, hymnal singing, and violin playing are sweeter than candy.

Illustrator's Dedication

For all the dogs who have made my life sweeter than candy.

Harvey liked to travel.

His first trip was to Grandpa's house in the woods.

He rested in Grandpa's deep overall pocket and breathed in the scent of peppermint candy while he waited for Grandpa to finish work and sit in the rocker.

Buddy licked his paws and waited too.

Creak. Creak. The rocker began to sway. Grandpa pulled Harvey out of his pocket and began to blow. Harvey sang a happy tune, a tune sweeter than candy.

Buddy sat up and howled.

Harvey frowned. Was the dog singing along, or was he howling to show how much he disliked Harvey's song? Whatever the reason, Harvey didn't like Buddy's howling.

One day, Grandpa said he didn't have enough breath to make his little harmonica sing, so he gave Harvey to Dad.

Harvey traveled to Dad's cabin by the creek. He peeked out the top of Dad's shirt pocket. Harvey sniffed and smiled. Dad's pocket smelled like chocolate cookies.

Dad patted his pocket and spoke to Buddy, "We'll see how Harvey sings for us tonight after dinner, shall we?"

Buddy wagged his tail.

Harvey didn't want to sing for Buddy. The dog slobbered, and he howled so loudly, he drowned out Harvey's song.

BUDDY

Squeak. Squeak. The porch swing began to move, and Dad reached for Harvey. Buddy jumped up and put his wet nose on Harvey's smooth front plate.

Yuck! Harvey didn't know how he could sing a happy tune, a tune sweeter than candy, with Buddy's nose in his face.

Dad began to blow, and Harvey began to sing. Buddy howled.

Harvey cried. He couldn't hear himself sing.

W.T.

Dad gave Harvey to his son, Walter, when he was old enough to take care of him. "Look, Son. I've carved your initials on Harvey. Everyone will know he belongs to you now. He'll fit just fine in your pocket."

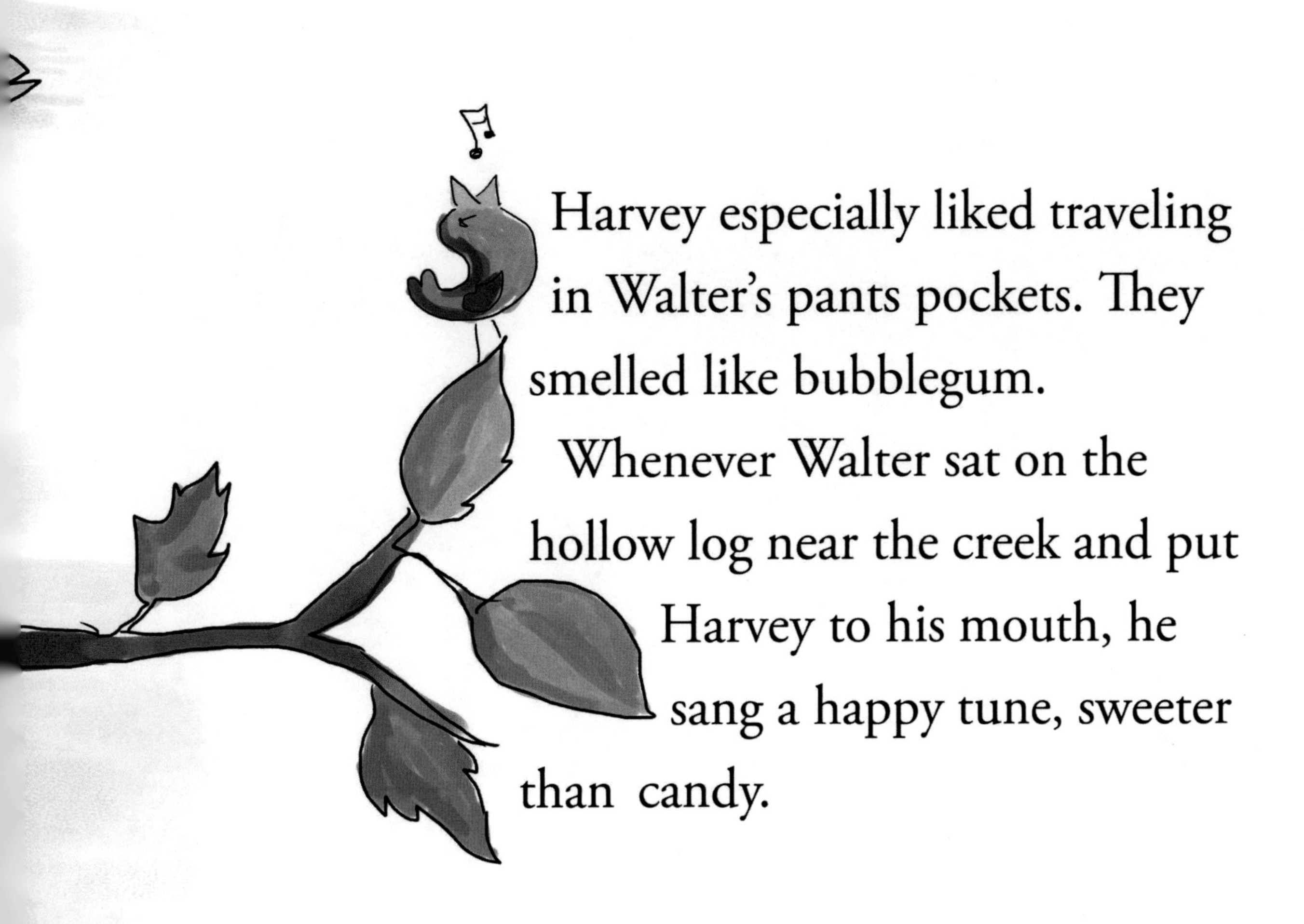

Harvey especially liked traveling in Walter's pants pockets. They smelled like bubblegum.

Whenever Walter sat on the hollow log near the creek and put Harvey to his mouth, he sang a happy tune, sweeter than candy.

Harvey liked living with Walter, Dad, and Mom, but not with Buddy. The dog swam or rolled in any water he found, so he always smelled damp and doggy. He also carried balls or other objects in his mouth wherever he went.

Harvey made a face. Not long ago, Walter pocketed one of Buddy's balls, forgetting Harvey traveled in the same pocket. Dog slobber soaked the entire ball. Double yuck!

Every time Harvey began to sing, and Buddy began to howl, the birds flew off.

A few times, when Harvey rested on a table near the sofa instead of in Walter's pockets, Buddy tried to sneak him out of the house. Harvey shook as he remembered his close calls.

Would Buddy have dug a hole and buried him in the yard like he did his bones? Would he have carried him around until he was so full of slobber he couldn't sing?

Thankfully, Walter saved him each time.

Why did Walter like Buddy anyway? His howling was not sweeter than candy.

W.T.
BUDDY

Sniff. Sniff. At that moment, as Harvey rested on the small table, he smelled dog. To his horror, Buddy came close. He opened his mouth and clamped his teeth around him.

"Stop! Put me back, Buddy. I like to travel, but not with you. Take me back to Walter."

But Buddy didn't listen. He trotted out the door.

Suddenly, everything went dark. Harvey choked and cried as dirt covered him.

"Buddy, take me to Walter. Please. I want to sing for him and smell his bubblegum pockets."

Harvey stayed in the dark for a long time before he heard Walter's voice.

"Find Harvey, Buddy."

Buddy barked and began digging. He picked Harvey up in his slobbery mouth and wagged his tail.

"Good boy." Walter patted Buddy's head and took Harvey.

Buddy smiled. Harvey didn't.

BBLE
GUM

Harvey liked to travel, but he didn't like bumping around in Walter's fishing wader's pocket. He slipped and slid and tried not to fall out. The pocket smelled damp and wormy.

Walter slipped on a rock, and Harvey fell from his pocket into the creek.

He landed with a splash then bounced and flipped as the water pushed him away from the bank.

"Harvey!" Walter reached for him, but the current moved him away from Walter's fingers into faster waters.

Harvey screamed, but water filled his mouth.

Walter raced along the bank beside him, Buddy barking at his heels.

No matter how hard he tried, he couldn't reach Harvey.

The little harmonica believed his singing days were over.

Walter pointed and yelled, "Buddy, get Harvey."

Harvey stopped crying.

Buddy plunged into the creek and swam toward him. Then he stuck his head in the water, opened his mouth, and grabbed Harvey.

"Good boy, Buddy." Harvey wished he had arms to pat the dog's nose.

BUDDY

“Good boy, Buddy.” Walter took Harvey and dried him with his sleeve.

Buddy shook, and more water landed on Harvey.

The little harmonica laughed. “I feel like singing.

BUDDY

Walter sat on the hollow log and pulled Harvey out of his pocket.

Buddy raised his snout to howl.

Harvey smiled. Maybe the dog was okay after all.

Harvey sang, and Buddy howled. Together, their duet sounded sweeter than candy.

Discussion Questions:

1. Why did Grandpa give Harvey to Dad?
2. Name the three pocket smells.
3. Why didn't Harvey like Buddy?
4. What were some things that happened to Harvey when Buddy snatched him away?
5. How did Harvey's feelings toward Buddy change?

Answers:

1. He didn't have enough breath to make Harvey sing.
2. Peppermint, chocolate cookies, and bubble gum.
3. He howled, slobbered, and smelled like wet dog.
4. Buddy got slobber on him and buried him in the dirt.
5. After Buddy rescued Harvey from the creek, Harvey decided the dog wasn't so bad after all. They became friends.

BUBBLE
GUM

Harvey and Buddy's Song

Tune: Are You Sleeping?

Where is Harvey? Where is Harvey?
Do you know? Do you know?
Buddy, won't you get him? Buddy won't you get him?
Find him now. Find him now.

Harvey's screaming, Harvey's screaming,
"Come get me. Come get me."
Buddy plunges in. Buddy plunges in.
The creek runs fast. The creek runs fast.

“Back to the log, back to the log,”
Walter calls. Walter calls.
“Let us sing a song. Let us sing a song.
Sit right down. Sit right down.”

Harvey and Buddy, Harvey and Buddy
Like to sing, like to howl,
Sweeter than candy, sweeter than candy,
All day long. All day long.

About the Author

Becky Van Vleet is a retired teacher and principal. She and her husband make their home in Colorado Springs where she enjoys spending time with her family, especially reading books to her grandchildren.

Becky has devoted her website to creating and preserving family memories and sharing family stories for the next generations. You can find her at: https://beckyvanvleet.com.

About the Illustrator

Courtney Smith lives in Franktown, Colorado, with her five children and her husband who is sweeter than candy. She does sports medicine, breeds Great Pyrenees puppies, and loves to scribble when she can. She has illustrated numerous children's picture books including *I Hate Oatmeal!*, *High-Water Hattie*, and *I Know What Grandma Does While I'm Napping*.

Made in the USA
Middletown, DE
09 May 2021

39165739R00029